Where Little Dog Gone?

Characters

Narrator

Boy

Dog

Girl

Man

Woman

Setting

A park, one day in spring

Picture Words

children

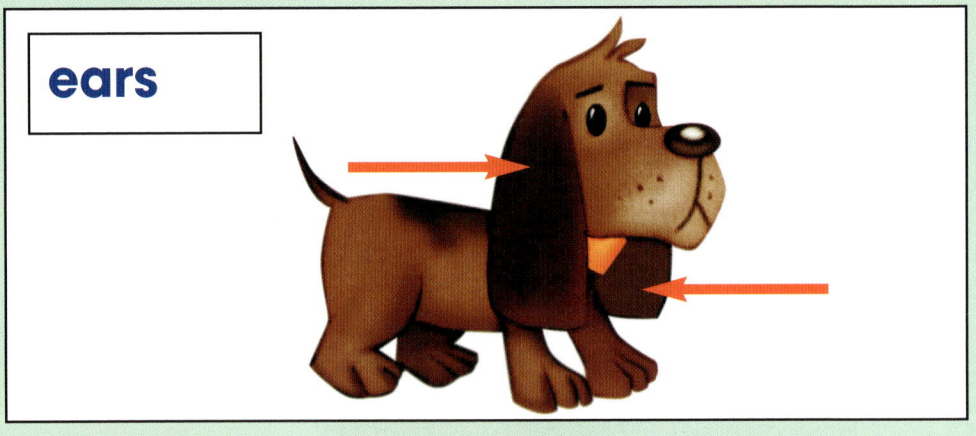

ears

Sight Words

| does | have | he | like |
| play | we | will | yes |

sad

tail

Enrichment Words

ball

find

long

short

**Narrator:** A boy and girl were in the park with their grandmother. They were playing with their dog.

**Boy:** Get the ball.

Dog: Woof!

 **Narrator:** The boy threw the ball. The dog ran after the ball.

 **Dog:** Woof, woof.

 **Narrator:** The dog ran far. The boy and girl could not find the dog.

 **Boy:** Dog! Dog! Where are you?

 **Girl:** Oh, where can he be?

 **Narrator:** The boy and girl asked a man and a woman for help.

 **Boy:** Have you seen a dog?

 **Man:** No.

 **Girl:** Have you seen a dog?

Woman: No.

 **Boy:** I am sad.

 **Girl:** I am very sad.

 **Man:** Do not be sad. We will help you.

 **Woman:** We will look. We will find the dog.

 **Man:** Is your dog big?

 **Boy:** No. The dog is little.

 **Woman:** Does your dog have long ears?

 **Girl:** No. The dog has short ears.

 **Man:** Does your dog have a long tail?

 **Boy:** Yes! The dog has a long tail.

 **Woman:** Does your dog like to play?

 **Girl:** Yes, the dog likes to play.

 **Man:** Does he like to play with a ball?

 **Boy:** Yes, he likes to play with a ball.

 **Woman:** Does he like to play with children?

 **Girl:** Yes! He likes children.

 **Woman:** Look! Your dog is there.

 **Dog:** Woof! Woof!

The End